W9-BJN-512

NOAH'S CATS AND THE DEVIL'S FIRE

Noah's Cats and the Devil's Fire

By Arielle North Olson

Illustrations by Barry Moser

Orchard Books   New York

Orchard Books
387 Park Avenue South
New York, NY 10016

Library of Congress Cataloging-in-Publication Data
Olson, Arielle North.
Noah's cats and the devil's fire / by Arielle North Olson;
illustrations by Barry Moser. p. cm.
Summary: A retelling of a traditional Romanian tale in which
the devil turns out to be the most troublesome passenger on
Noah's ark.
ISBN 0-531-05984-7. ISBN 0-531-08584-8 (lib. bdg.)
[1. Folklore—Romania.] I. Moser, Barry, ill. II. Wakeman,
Thomas H., date. III. Title.
GB458.8.S95 1991 333.91'7—dc20 91-17408

2 4 6 8 10 9 7 5 3 1

To our present-day Noahs,

Christy, Kevin, Caitlin, Lindsey, and Ian

—A.N.O.

And for Isabelle Rose

—B.M.

Author's Note:
There is no devil aboard the biblical Noah's Ark
(Genesis 6–8), but the devil is Noah's most troublesome
passenger in this Rumanian folktale.
Noah's Cats and the Devil's Fire *grew out of a variation of the*
Noah story found in Rumanian Bird and Beast Stories *by*
M. Gaster (London: Sidgwick & Jackson, Ltd., 1915).

NOAH'S CATS AND THE DEVIL'S FIRE

Long, long ago

a gigantic flood was about to cover the earth. So Noah built a mighty ark. And the minute he finished, guess what happened? The devil himself came striding up the gangplank.

Noah's cats hissed, but the devil brushed right past them.

"I'm going with you," he said, bold as you please.

Noah looked him over, from the tips of his horns to the end of his pointed tail.

"Oh, no, you're not," said Noah, and he clapped his hands. "Begone!"

This made the devil furious. He spat fire and stamped his cloven hooves. He slashed his tail through the air, and puffs of smoke shot out of his ears.

And what did Noah's cats do then? They jumped on Noah's shoulders and snarled right back.

Noah laughed.

Just think how the devil felt! He glowered at Noah with fiery red eyes and leaned so close to him that their noses almost touched. The cats could hardly stand the sizzling heat.

But Noah didn't even blink. "Off you go," he said.

The devil stormed down the gangplank, gnashing his teeth and muttering to himself.

"No one can keep me off," he growled.

And believe it or not, the devil was right.

When the animals came aboard, two by two, a pair of fiery eyes peered out from under the lion's mane—the fiery red eyes of the devil who had turned himself into a mouse.

The minute that devil-mouse was safely past Noah, he slid down the lion's tail and hid behind some hay. Then he waited for a chance to make trouble. And while he waited, the very last animals hopped and trotted and slithered and scuttled aboard.

Noah looked over his list and smiled. "Everyone's here," he said.

"Me too," the devil-mouse cackled, ever so quietly—but not quietly enough.

And who was listening? Noah's cats. They

pussyfooted toward the pile of hay. But the devil-mouse just twitched his whiskers and disappeared into the shadows.

Just then dark clouds began to gather, far off on the horizon. Noah and his sons rushed to haul in the gangplank. And their wives raced from the deck to the hold, leading animals into their stalls.

And the cats? They leaped to the railing so no one would step on their tails.

When the deck was finally cleared, Noah watched the storm clouds rolling in. A few drops of water splashed on the ark. Then the winds blew. And suddenly the rain was pouring down. Noah ran for shelter, the cats at his heels. Lightning flashed and thunder roared and buckets of water pounded on the roof. The great flood was on its way.

Day after day, Noah and his family cared for the animals—feeding them, giving them fresh water, and whispering in their ears when thunder boomed around the ark.

And day after day, the devil-mouse tried to think of ways to cause trouble.

Early one morning he tickled the laughing hyenas, set the donkeys braying, and tugged at the lions' tails until they roared. No one could sleep.

Noah just sat up and stretched. "It must be time to feed those animals."

The devil-mouse gritted his teeth—but soon he thought of something else.

When no one was looking, that fiery creature took a swim in Noah's washbowl. He left the water steaming, with a thin scum of dirt and mouse hair.

Noah only noticed that the water was warm. "How nice," he said. "I wonder who did it?"

The devil-mouse thrashed his tail and thought again.

He waited until the cats were napping. Then he gnawed holes in the feed sacks and scattered grain all over the floor.

Noah didn't mind. "Someone's already fed the chickens and ducks," he said. "Good. I'll take care of the pigs."

Well, the devil-mouse was furious, because nothing he did bothered Noah. He stormed across the ark, cursing and scratching and biting at anything in his way. Then he dashed to the deck and jumped up on the railing.

Rain still poured from the sky, and the water crept higher and higher. There was no land as far as he could see.

And that is when an idea hit the devil-mouse, an idea so evil he shook with fiendish laughter—

and fell right off the slippery railing. But wouldn't you know it, he landed safely on the deck.

Well, the devil-mouse didn't lose a moment. He picked himself up, raced to the ladder, and scrambled to the bottom of the ark. Then he crouched low and began to chew—watching all the while for the cats.

If he could make a hole, water would rush in. The ark would sink down, down, down to the bottom of the sea, and all the creatures would drown.

There would be no more pandas. No more horses. No more chickens or camels or cats. And no more Noah.

The devil-mouse gnawed at the thick wooden plank. And bit by bit, the hole grew.

At first no one noticed him chewing. But one day four beady eyes spied on him from the shad-

ows. The devil-mouse smiled wickedly. If he could get Noah's mice to help, they could make a hole faster.

So the devil-mouse called to the other two. His voice sounded harsh, but Noah's mice crept from behind a barrel to see what he was doing.

And *that* is where the devil-mouse made his mistake.

Noah might not have noticed the beginning of a mouse hole. He might not have seen bits of wood on the floor.

But Noah *did* notice three mice.

THREE?? He knew all the creatures had come aboard *two by two.*

Noah lunged for the devil-mouse. He shouted for his cats. One cat chased the devil-mouse around the barrel. The other took a deep breath

and pounced the moment the devil-mouse flew by. In one big gulp, she gobbled him up, fiery eyes and all.

Imagine how hot the cat felt with the devil-mouse inside. She raced up the ladder to the deck and leaped onto the railing. Then she spat the devil-mouse into the sea. And with a flash of light, the mouse turned into a viper fish and swam away.

So Noah's cats saved the ark and everyone inside. Soon the flood went down, and they all walked again on the face of the earth.

But there was something different about the cat who had pounced on the devil. Did that red-hot demon leave a bit of fire inside her?

Ever after, her fur made sparks when Noah petted her—and her eyes gleamed in the dark. And that's the way it is with cats to this very day.

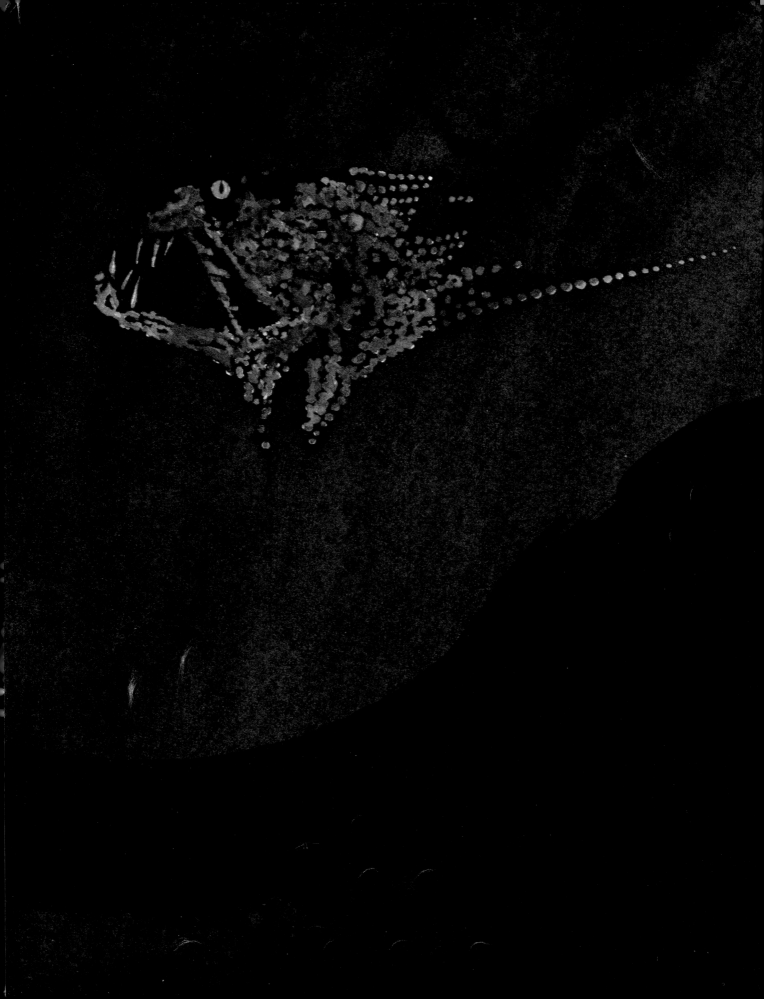

Manufactured in the United States of America
Printed by General Offset Company, Inc.
Bound by Horowitz/Rae
Book design by Barry Moser

The text of this book is set in 16 point Trump Medieval,
designed by Georg Trump.
The illustrations are transparent watercolor painted on paper
handmade by Simon Green at The Hayle Mill,
Maidstone, Kent, G.B.
The calligraphy is by Reassurance Wunder, based on sixteenth-
century forms designed by Giovano Battista Palatino and
Giovanniantonio Tagliente.